ALLIGATORS
ALL AROUND

AN ALPHABET

ALLIGATORS ALL AROUND

by
MAURICE SENDAK

AN ALPHABET

HarperTrophy

A Division of HarperCollins*Publishers*

 alligators all around

B

bursting balloons

C catching colds

D

doing dishes

E entertaining elephants

F forever fooling

G getting giggles

 having headaches

 imitating Indians

J

juggling jelly beans

K

keeping kangaroos

L

looking like lions

M making macaroni

N never napping

O ordering oatmeal

P pushing people

Q quite quarrelsome

 riding reindeer

 shockingly spoiled

T throwing tantrums

U

usually upside down

V very vain

 wearing wigs

X

x-ing x's

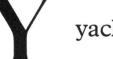 yackety-yacking

 Zippity zound!
Alligators ALL around.